To everyone I've ever known
    who's had a **"bugbear"** of their own.
From line-jumpers to summer rain,
    to standing-room only on the train ~ P.H.

To Angel, for being there ~ C.S.

tiger tales
5 River Road, Suite 128, Wilton, CT 06897
Published in the United States 2017
Originally published in Great Britain 2017
by Little Tiger Press
Text by Patricia Hegarty
Text copyright © 2017 Little Tiger Press
Illustrations copyright © 2017 Carmen Saldaña
ISBN-13: 978-1-68010-053-2
ISBN-10: 1-68010-053-X
Printed in China
LTP/1400/1690/0816
10 9 8 7 6 5 4 3 2 1

For more insight and activities,
visit us at www.tigertalesbooks.com

BUG BEAR

by Patricia Hegarty

Illustrated by Carmen Saldaña

tiger tales

Down in the forest,
    Bear started to doze,
When a small stripy bug
    came and sat on his nose.

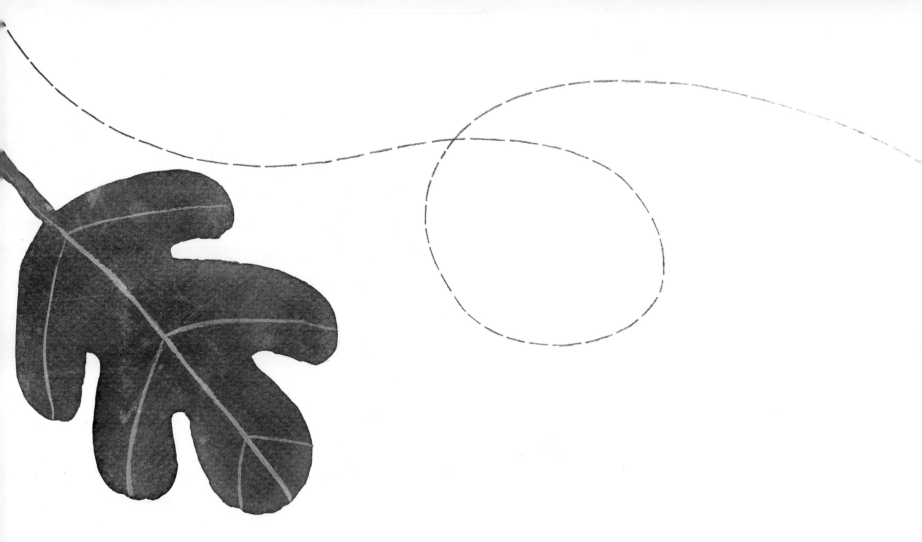

"Good day to you, Bear. I'm just passing through,
Looking for lodgings . . .
    and I've chosen YOU!"

Bear lifted his head and opened one eye,
Then closed it again with a world-weary sigh.

But Bug wasn't easy
for Bear to ignore.

He whirred
and he buzzed
and then buzzed
a bit more.

"You're so soft and squishy
and cuddly, dear Bear—
And you DO have a lot
of that warm fur to spare."

"Not listening! Not listening! Don't care what you say!
My fur's not your home. Now PLEASE go away!"

"But your fur is so fuzzy, so soft, and so snug—
It's just perfect bedding for a little ol' bug!"

Bug looped the loop,
then he sat on Bear's snout.
"Come now, my friend. Let's both hug it out."

"I don't want to hug you, you fluttering pest.
Why can't you see that I'm trying to **rest!**"

"You're SO funny, Bear,"
said Bug with a giggle.
And he nestled right down
with a jiggly wiggle.

"Stop tickling!" Bear cried. "I'm tired of you!
Why must you cause such a hullabaloo?"

Bear stomped and he clomped
and jumped up and down.

He swished and he swatted,
then said with a frown . . .

"Oh, troublesome bug,
why on earth pick on me?
And not one of these OTHER fine

creatures you see?"

"Grumpy?!" said Bear.
"GRUMPY, you say?!

"I'll give you grumpy—
you've ruined my day!"

"Won't SOMEBODY
help me?"
cried Bear with a howl.

"Can I be of service?"
asked clever old Owl.

"Oh, Owl," whimpered Bear, "please tell him from me,
He's GOT to buzz off and just let me be!"

"Don't worry," said Owl, "for I have a plan.
Bear *can't* be your bed, but *I* know who can.
My friend is just perfect—I'm sure you'll agree.
He's soft and he's hanging
up there in that tree."

"Well, why, oh, why
I'm all ears," said Bug

"All right," said Owl
I'd like you to

idn't you say so before?
You must tell me more!"

don't get in a froth.
eet my furry friend, Sloth."

"I'd be MOST grateful," said Sloth with a grin,
"To have a small bug make his home on my skin.
I don't move around much because I'm so slow.
But now I'll have a friend wherever I go!"